INSIDE THE CUP

Life inside the world's most popular coffee shop

AARON PITRE

AARON PITRE
www.aaronpitre.com

Printed in the United States of America

First Printing 2014
First Edition 2014
Second Printing 2021
Second Edition 2021
ISBN 978-1-7359169-3-4
10 9 8 7 6 5 4 3 2

For the baristas, waiters, retail sales associates,
cashiers, and bus drivers of the world.

For any human being who has had to
serve another human being.

The Captains

Cosmo Schwartz
60, CEO and Founder of the Cosmos Coffee Cup.

Danny
25, a recent college graduate with dual Master's Degrees.

Al
20s, a captain at a Cosmos Coffee Cup on a college campus.

Sonia
None of your business, a captain who hates Christmas.

Bijoux
40, a doctor from Haiti.

Randy
Old enough, a captain from a small town in the south.

Sage
Ageless, a new-age captain who breaks company rules.

Ronnie
30s, a longtime captain who has big dreams.

Table of Contents

Prologue

(Lights up. We see a video of Cosmo Schwartz, a charismatic CEO, projected on a screen. He smiles then speaks.)

Cosmo: Dear captains, today, on the thirtieth anniversary of the Cosmos Coffee Cup, a.k.a "The Cup," we sit proudly atop the market as the biggest and most popular coffee shop in the entire universe. We operate over 50,000 state-of-the-art stores worldwide, but we never would have made it this far without you. Thanks to your stellar work and astronomical dedication, we are transforming humankind, one cup at a time, with "coffee that is out of this world."

As our captains know well, the Cosmos Coffee Cup experience begins the very moment a customer sees our store sign, a three-dimensional projection of a rotating spiral galaxy. The logo of our brand, and a reminder to all of humanity that no matter what we look like, or where we come from, we all are stars in the sky. That is why our beverages come in *"Giant," "Nova," and "Supernova."*

Upon store entry, our customers leave the current world behind to embark on a journey to what we at The Cup call the *Fifth Dimension*: a place not bound by the four dimensions of work, home, time, and space.

1

A total-immersion micro-verse. A plane of existence... beyond, where nothing matters but the full satisfaction of the senses.

I call you my "captains," because you are navigators of new and exciting territories, who come to work knowing that every day brings a mission to blast off far above the call of duty, and give every customer a cosmic experience. That is the purpose of The Cup's existence, and anytime I visit one of our stores, I am moved to tears, not because you have brought my vision to life or because you have made my wildest dreams come true, but because I get to see firsthand how you are making the world a better place each time you honor our mission. For that, I thank you from the bottom of my heart... and beyond.

It should come as no surprise that last year was our best year in company history. We turned record profits for The Cup, so to express my gratitude for all your hard work, your pay is being doubled and your lunch break is being increased to one hour.

Here's to you, my beloved captains. You are the heart and soul of The Cup. Keep up the good work, keep kicking ass-teroid, and as we say to all of our customers in the Fifth Dimension: *"Have a nice voyage."*

Yours Truly,

Cosmo Schwartz.
Better known as... *Uncle Cosmo.*

> *(Blackout. Space-age music plays. The screen projects a spiral galaxy as stars are projected all over the stage.)*

Act One

Scene 1

(Enter Danny. Stars and music fade out. Lights up.)

Danny: Hello. I'm Danny. Remember my name and remember the expression on my face. The eyes that have a fresh, new twinkle, the proudly-flared nostrils that are sucking in more air, and the soft, luscious lips revealing a smile that now shows off extra teeth. You are looking at someone who made it. Today is Monday, but I will forever remember it as my day, my first day with a real job in over two years. I am incredibly grateful.

If hell exists, I'm pretty sure it would look and feel like hunting for a job in this economy. I do accept responsibility for a portion of the pain because I guess I shouldn't have overestimated my credentials while simultaneously underestimating how truly difficult it is to get on solid ground during these times. But if you allow me less than a minute to explain, you will, at least, understand why I made my mistake.

You see, until recently, I fancied myself a dynamic go-getter with plenty of talent, experience, and drive to offer to the world. And where obstacles had frequently found them -selves standing in my way, it was the aforementioned

7

qualities that gave me the fists to fight until I won.

If you had a copy of my resume in front of you right now, it would read that I am a well-educated professional who has earned two master's degrees in French and Art History. What my resume *wouldn't* tell you, however, is that my degrees might as well be participation trophies at this point in time because they haven't led to shit, pardon my French.

I have literally gone everywhere in this city in search of jobs only to learn, the hard way, that there aren't many available anywhere. And if the scarcity of employment opportunities for young college graduates trying to get on their feet wasn't aggravating enough, the fact that I have had to jump through hoops to compete for the few jobs that *were* available has brought me to the edge. Who knew low-points had edges?

Take when I tried to get a job as a dishwasher at OMG Thursdays for example. For some strange reason, a college degree was required to even apply. How a college education bears relation to washing dishes is beyond me, but beggars can't be choosers, especially when you have to persuade the choosers to choose you, so I followed every instruction of the application process, which was nothing short of over-the-top.

Step one. The lovely OMG Thursday's team required all aspiring dishwashers submit a resume and cover letter along with their application. And you better believe I really sold myself on my materials as a dedicated, professional longtime dishwasher. I briefly considered changing the job title to *"Dishwasheur,"* you know, ending in an "eur" instead of the common and standard "er" because I thought it sounded fancy and might give me the edge over other applicants who, given the current state of affairs in this country, very well could also have two master's degrees, or PhDs, or even worse, degrees in medicine. But since I was in no position to take a risk, I kept things straightforward to improve my chances of making it to the next step, which I did.

For step two, I had to take a multiple-choice test with a #2 pencil that I was asked, ahead of time, to provide. It was very important that I made sure I took a #2... I mean *used* a #2 on my test, or the machine grading my test might fail me on the spot. Failure, of course, would mean no job, neither would passing the test for that matter, but I would move on to the next step, which I'm proud to say I did because I passed the test with flying colors. I must also say, for your information, that the test was surprisingly difficult, as I hadn't expected it to include math, history and science questions, nor had I expected it to be *timed.*

If you're lucky enough to still be standing after steps one

and two, you'll finally get to the fun part; step three; the pleasure of having to submit to a credit check that you must pass with a score of at least 700, and then, *finally* then, you'll be ready to *interview* for the job. You heard that correctly, all of that just for an interview, which I didn't get because my credit is bad thanks to six figures of student debt; a situation that is neither new nor surprising to me. I experienced the same outcome when I applied to sell cosmetics at Tracy's department store: *rejection on the basis of credit.* Exactly how do the creditors expect me to pay off my debt without a job... that I'm not able to get because of my debt... that I won't be able to pay off without a job?!

At this point in time, I'm pretty sure I would need a bachelor's degree in volunteerism to volunteer to clean the piss and poop off city street corners. And I would probably need a master's degree in ass-wipery to wipe the asses of said piss-and-poopers! And you bet your ass I'd do it with a megawatt smile because it would mean my degrees were going to *some* use.

I decided to switch things up and "expand my horizons" by trying a new method for job hunting, which I called *"searching for employment opportunities anywhere I could fucking find them,"* pardon my French. I turned every stone looking for a job! I'm talking organic dog food taste-testing, inflatable man repairs, and lizard-sitting. You name it, I applied for it. But even with a new attitude, old patterns persisted, and all my efforts to find gainful employment have left me empty handed, hungry, and lost.

I was just about to give up, when, miraculously, I was offered a job at the Cosmos Coffee Cup on Second Avenue, here in Pine City. All it took was an *application* and an *interview*, and voila, my life is turning around. And while I can't say that I'm fully back on track, I'm definitely taking a step in the right direction. For starters, the pay is... good —enough, there are *great* benefits, and get this: my store just so happens to be down the street from the French Embassy! So, I've hatched a new, three-phase plan.

Phase one: I'll meet some customers here at The Cup who work for the embassy, and would have a job for me.

Phase two: I'll work both jobs, make enough money to move out of the library at my alma mater, and get a place of my own.

Phase three: I'll quit my job at The Cup and work full-time at the embassy! And then my job at the embassy could lead to a job in France, and in France I could find my way into a job as an art dealer, or an art buyer, or a museum curator, and all the greatest works of art would pass through me *en route* to their homes around the world! That has always been a dream of mine, and this job at The Cup could give me that chance. I mean, *something* has to and I think I deserve it. In fact, I *know* I deserve it because I always did what I was told, the way I was told was right.

Did I not follow the blueprint laid out to us by our parents, and their parents, and their parents? When they *all* said *"go to school, get a degree, and you will get a good job,"* I believed them.

They told us everywhere, every day, on TV, in the news, ads, and countless billboards littering the highway, that as long as you do what you're told and follow the blueprint, you can't fail. "Your American dream will come true by the skin of your teeth and the straps of your boots." But I guess some concepts, like resumes, sound great on paper, but when it's time to put them to the test, on your feet, they don't always work... so *you* don't work.

But it's all good now. *C'est bon*. I've got a new job and a new plan! And I firmly believe it'll work *as planned,* as long I don't do anything to fuck it up...

(Lights dim. Music plays. Lights up on Danny, now standing at the Command Center. They proceed to reenact each customer encounter as they describe it.)

I fucked it up. I mean I really fucked it up, pardon my French. It all started this morning with my first customer ever at The Cup, a woman who ordered an *Iced Supernova Tektite Tea*... and nearly was charged $100,000 for it because I hit the wrong button on my screen at the *Command Center,* where customers place their orders, no big deal, right? Wrong!

I had to start over by keying in her order again, and as I was swiping her credit card, I knocked over her cup of iced tea. Do you have any idea how much liquid can fit inside a Supernova-sized cup? A tidal wave of black tea, raspberry, lemon, and hibiscus engulfed the woman, covered the floor, and soaked a few customers who were standing behind her, waiting in a line... that was beginning to stretch out the door.

My second customer ever was a man who came up to me and started barking like a dog *(they imitate the customer)*: *WOOF WOOF WOOF WOOF WOOF!*

I just stood there, looking at him, barking away as if he expected me to speak fluent dog, with no clue as to what I should do. I locked eyes with a service dog in the store and, for a split second, was very hopeful that the lovely pooch might be able to help me figure out what Winston was saying. However, the look in their sweet little eyes said it all:

"Don't look at me."

Luckily, a moment later, I found out from my co-captain that the barking man was named Winston, and when Winston barked, it meant he wanted a *Nova Flying Strawberry Saucer*, with all the accoutrements on it; it's a medium strawberry milkshake topped with whipped cream and strawberry "plasma," but if he howls, then hold the whipped cream. So, I placed his order. He didn't howl, but he did start barking at me, very loud and super fast *(they imitate a loud, fast dog bark)*. He was clearly irritated by something, but I didn't know what, and then I remembered that he paid with a twenty dollar bill, and I forgot to give him his change! No worries.

I said *"Sorry, Sir! I forgot to give you your change. Just one second,..."* but our new Command Center prohibits captains from opening the cash crater once a transaction is complete,... so I said *"Sorry, Sir. I just need to wait until the next customer pays, and then I'll be able to give you your change,"* no big deal, right? Wrong...

Well, the next customer's tongue was burned. All because I forgot to specify that his *Hot Chocolate Chondrite* was supposed to be a "*Not-Too-Hot Chocolate Chondrite*." He spent the next ten minutes simultaneously putting ice on his tongue, and threatening to "kick my *ath*." Not to mention, Winston the Dog Man had been waiting for his change the whole time! When I gave it to him, he growled at me.

(Lights dim. Music plays. Lights up on Danny, now in the bathroom.)

Danny: Break time. Locking myself in the customer restroom just might be the best decision ever because it is UNREAL. The glowing walls and ambient music are giving me all the chill vibes I so desperately need right now. I cannot think of a more perfect location to have a good, long, self-pitying cry before I quit and get the hell out of here.

As I sit down on the toilet to cry, it beeps and I think *"Oh great, now I've broken the toilet!"* But then the lights grow dim...

(Lights fade slowly to black. The screen displays space imagery as Danny describes it)

...as the mirror turns into this screen, projecting a three -dimensional image of a spaceship traveling past all these fluorescent planets and glowing asteroids... and I know that this is not just another fuck-up, pardon my French. This is on purpose.

Out of nowhere, I hear this booming voice say *(they imitate an echoing, deep voice)*:

"All things known were once unknown... unknown... unknown... Have courage... courage..., and explore... explore... explore..."

And then, like magic, the bathroom resets to normal.

(Lights up. The screen fades back to black.)

It is easily one of the coolest things I've ever seen in my life... and it's making me think.

For the last four hours, I've been living my biggest nightmare, ruining a job, and squandering a chance I really need by screwing everything up... yet somehow I'm surviving. I mean, I haven't been fired yet, and if I take a moment to breathe and really think about how today has been going so far, I realize... it could be worse. This is just day one, after all. Who told me I had to be perfect right from the start? Or at all?

Here I am, presently employed, on a lunch break, with my workday half behind me, and two choices fully in front of me. Either I go forth, through the mistakes and embarrassment, into the unknown, or... I turn around,

16

leave,... and go back to a failed plan. If I've already hit rock bottom, what more do I have to lose? And if my perfect plans failed, could it mean a bigger plan is at work for me, you know? Something that I can't really see right now from where I am? Maybe.

I've made my decision. After hearing so many "nos" in life, I think I'm going to take a chance on "maybe."

(Lights fade. Music plays. Lights up on Danny, now in the Captain's Quarters.)

Danny: I'm Danny. Remember my name and remember my face. You are looking at someone who survived their first day of work at The Cup. It was a total disaster, but I've decided to stay and see what happens.

On my way to the Captain's Quarters, excuse me, "CQ" to clock out and go home, I find Mary, my commander, waiting for me at her pod. I'm convinced she is going to "kick my ath." But to my surprise, she actually commends me on my great work... *excusez moi*? She tells me (*as Mary*):

"Something's always being messed up at The Cup, but don't worry about it. You'll get used to the swing of things quickly, and then your job will become fun. (Danny smiles) I promise."

I think she might be right. And to be honest, I have to say today *was* actually... kind of... fun! In its own drink-spilling, growling, tongue-burning kind of way! And there's no denying these stores are AMAZING! I mean, look at this place! Who gets to say they work from the observation deck of a giant spaceship floating through the Universe? And that restroom? Holy crap, no pun intended. I could have stayed in there *AAAALLLLLLLLLL* day.

So today, with your blessing, I think I'll stop believing in mistakes, because it's pretty difficult to fear something you don't believe in, and as for little mess-ups here and there, it's okay! I'm human, and shit happens! Pardon my French.

And hey, who knows? Maybe I can find my way to France through The Cup. Yeah! They have a Cosmos Coffee Cup in Paris. Maybe I can transfer there, after I've worked here for a while, and then I could use my experience at *Le Cup* in Paris to open my own *cafe des artistes* in the heart of the City of Lights. And maybe I'll meet and romance a beautiful Parisian... and we'll get married, and adopt two beautiful French children. And we'll name them "Maude" and "Claude" because those names sound similar enough in French and English and that way both sides of the family won't have any trouble pronouncing their names.

Or maybe... in Paris, my plans will completely fall apart and

I'll fail again, this time in the middle of the most romantic city in the world... and somehow, in the midst of failure, I'll be happy... because that's all I really want... and you know what? Right now... I am. So, since I'm a bonafide Cosmos Coffee Cup captain now, I want to tell all of you to have a nice voyage. Bon Voyage!

(Blackout. Space-age music plays. The screen projects a spiral galaxy as stars are projected all over the stage. Exit Danny.)

Scene 2

(Enter Al. Lights up. Stars and music fade out.)

Al: S'up. I'm Al. I work at The Cup at Central University, in Orange Bay, but I'm not a student. People ask me that a lot around here.

I started working here when I moved to the area a few years back. You see, I live just down the street, so I thought it would be hella convenient to work close to home because... are you ready for this?... I don't have a car!!!! I know, shocking right? I mean, who doesn't have a car this day and age? And in Orange Bay too!

But that's just me. I prefer to walk whenever and wherever I can. This includes anytime I have to move to a new place, which is totally cool with me because I'm a minimalist. I can literally put everything I own into a backpack, or better yet pile everything on top of my head, and move, just like I did when I moved here... on foot... which took me about two months. I highly recommend you try it because there's no better way to see the beauty of this amazing country than by walking across it. Don't even bother to make a plan, just walk until you feel like stopping, then chill for a bit. Then, when you feel like moving again, pile your stuff on top of your head and start walking again. Then, when you find somewhere you like, stay. That's how I got here.

So, I work on a college campus, right? It's, like, a place to go for higher learning, where you're supposed to feed your mind and grow more intelligent, right? Like, college is supposed to make you smarter, right? So then... like, where are all the smart people? Seriously, like, where did they go? Because, at this store, I only see about five a day, six or seven tops... and the rest of 'em are friggin' idiots, I swear!

Lemme ask you a serious question. Like, how do you order something, pay me, then totally forget what just happened? Or, how do you come in, *every day*, order the same thing, *every day*, go through the same routine, *every day*, and still not know where to pick up your drink? For, like, the five-thousandth time, homie, it'll be ready for you over there! The same place that you got your drink from yesterday, and the day before that, and the day before that, and the day before that. What the hell? Are you using all of your brain power for your classes? Do you even know where your classes are? No, for real! That's, like, a serious question, because every day it's, like, a real struggle for you to find a cup on a counter just six feet away from you, and it's really starting to scare me. It might help if you GOT OFF THE PHONE!!!! Or, maybe you should... you know... stay off the drugs. Bro, you should try it! But I know you won't.

21

Instead, you'll come into my store drunk, or high as fuck, asking me if I want to *"partayyyyyyy,"* with your stank breath smelling like Mad Dog 20/20... and you'll give me shit when I ask you to leave. But bro, I'm only asking you to leave because you're being too loud, so be a quiet drunk, and you can stay! Aren't they supposed to teach you that in college?

But seriously, I don't blame you for thinking every friggin' day is "Thirsty Thursday" because this whole friggin' campus is a friggin' frat house, and that includes this shitshow of a coffee shop! So, carry on, I guess. And if you keep on partying as hard as you do, you might be perfect for a job here.

(Lights fade. Music plays. Lights up on Al, now in the Captain's Quarters.)

Al: I friggin' hate my co-captains. They all suck balls. They're always showing up to work a few hours late and leaving a few hours early—provided they haven't already called out because they're *"not feelin' it."* And on the days when they actually *do* show up for work, the quality of the work they *do* do on the job is *doo doo!*

Every day, I lowkey expect to see this store closed down or burnt to the friggin' ground. And if the alcoholism weren't bad enough, everyone who works here pretends to be best friends, so everyone can learn everything about everybody and constantly talk shit about one another behind their backs! I have never worked with a bigger bunch of two-faced shitheads in my life! And in the style of my workplace, I admit... that I'd probably never tell them that to their faces. Not because I don't want to, believe me, I do, but because it'd be too much trouble.

You see, our entire store culture is dictated to us from the top down by our sorry excuse for a store commander, Skylar. With a name like *Sky*-lar, you'd think he was born to work at The Cup. But no, he sucks balls too. He might as well be one of my co-captains at this point. I mean, he practically is. He went to school here, and totally runs the store based on who he likes. I'm on his good side for now, I think, but he has been a real asshole to everyone lately... including our customers.

Like, a couple of days ago, a customer came in and asked *(speaking as customer)*:

"Um, what's a Milky Way Latte?"

She was a young woman, probably a freshman because she seemed to be so green, you know what I mean? I didn't get the impression that she'd done a lot of things on her own.

So, in response to her question, Skylar mimics her voice and says *(speaking as Skylar, imitating the customer)*:

"Umm... It's a drink. Everything you need to know is right there on the menu."

And of course my co-captains laughed, because they thought it was *"like, the funniest thing ev-ar,"* and I'm pretty sure I saw tears forming in the eyes of that young customer... but I'll never know for sure because she made a beeline for the door and left, without ordering anything, probably never to come back to this store again.

I felt bad for the girl, you know? I wanted to go outside and ask her if she was okay. I mean, the semester had only just started. Maybe this whole college experience was really new to her. Maybe she was a little overwhelmed, and just wanted something to drink to help her keep her day going, and we embarrassed her... and there was nothing I could do... no matter how badly I wanted to do something. And since I didn't do anything, did that mean I was part of the problem? Shit really pissed me off, you know? To think that this was what a college environment had become. A friggin' high school. Well, that was strike one for me.

(Lights fade. Music plays. Lights up on Al, now standing at the Command Center.)

24

Al: Okay, so we just hired a new girl here, right? Her name's Rene. Rene's cool. She's a sweet girl, but she's super slow at taking orders. I don't really mind, though, because she's always upbeat, on-time, and she seems to really like the job. Everyone's super nice to her to her face... but she has no idea how much shit my co-captains talk about her behind her back. They think she's dumber than rocks, nobody wants to work with her, and they all make fun of her, which I don't even understand because all of my co-captains would probably get lost in the storage closet, excuse me, the *utility chamber,* if the door were closed, so compared to the sample group, Rene's actually a friggin' genius.

My co-captains have the dumbest friggin' nickname for Rene; they call her "The Abyss," because they think there's nothing but a deep, cavernous, empty space between her ears *(Al rolls their eyes).* Rene doesn't know that's what they call her, even though they'll say things around her like *"Hey Rene, you should stream The Abyss on Netflix."*

They figure she's too stupid to know they're making fun of her, and since Rene always laughs *with* them, it seems like she might be. I don't really know Rene's story because she's on the quieter side, but since I wouldn't ever volunteer to have conversations with these assholes, it's a wise move on her part, dumb or not.

So here we all are, dys-functioning as usual. Today is Tuesday, and we're all prepared for our morning meteor shower. That's what all Cosmos Coffee Cup captains call a morning rush. On my left, we have my co-captain, Johnny a.k.a. "12-pack Johnny (and I'm not talking about his abs)" at the *Thermo Lab:* the area where all hot beverages are made; On my right, Commander Skylar at the *Cold Lab:* where all cold beverages are made; In the center, yours truly, holding command at the *Brewing Space Station:* where all drip coffee and tea are brewed; To the front, we have Alexa who is only an hour late and mildly hungover today, taking orders at *Command Center Two*, and at *Command Center One,* we have... Rene, The Abyss, taking orders *very* slowly.

Skylar's in classic form today. He says *(speaking as Skylar)*:

"Hey Rene, I want you to ring up the next customers as slowly as you can."

Rene says *(speaking as Rene)*:

"Ummm Okay,"

and goes back to ringing up customers, only now she's moving *(Al imitates Rene's movements)* in slow motion.

Everyone is laughing at her, except me, and now Johnny has

taken out his phone to start recording Rene. Alexa and Skylar are laughing uncontrollably now, just howling, and this, of course, catches Rene's attention. So, she turns around and asks them *(speaking as Rene)*:

"What's so funny?"

And Johnny says *(speaking as Johnny)*:

"Umm... we were just watching dumb people fail."

This is STRIKE TWO for me. Rene says *(speaking as Rene)*:

"that doesn't sound funny..."

So, Commander Skylar chimes in and says *(speaking as Skylar)*:

"I'm sure you'd know."

I think Rene knows at this point that people are making fun of her, so she just kind of smiles and goes back to taking orders at a quicker pace... and this is STRIKE THREE for me! "It" has been had. So I grab the microphone that we use to announce orders that are ready, and say:

"Speaking of dumb people failing, Johnny, why don't you show Rene the video where you stuck a roman candle in your butt and burned your asshole?"

The entire store takes a collective gasp, Johnny's face turns a gorgeous shade of brick red, he runs to the back room, and Skylar is ripshit! He yells at me *(speaking as Skylar)*:

"Dude, what's your friggin' problem?"

Finally, I can tell him the truth to his face:

"Dude, my friggin' problem is that you're all a bunch of two-faced bullies, who act like babies, and I'm sick of this bullshit. I'm sick of everyone talking shit behind everyone's back, and I'm sick of you acting like you're still an undergrad! You're almost forty years old. Grow up, and learn how to run a fucking store, Dude!"

Now Skylar starts to cry, saying that he thought I was *(speaking as Skylar)*:

"...like, cooler than that,"

and that he *(speaking as Skylar)*:

"...like, actually liked me so, like, why would I act like that?"

He also lets me know that I am an asshole and a loser, and that I'm FIRED! Sur-friggin-prise!!!!

Honestly, I feel relieved. I hate this store and everyone in it. I grab my things from CQ, but before I leave, I storm back on the floor, right to Command Center One, and tell Rene everything; how people made fun of her, about her nickname, how she's a little slow at the Command Center, and how I wanted to tell her this before I left... everything! She thanks me and says *"I know."*

I say *"You knew all along?"* And she says *(speaking as Rene)*

"Yeah, I'm not dumb! I just don't care. People will talk, but it doesn't matter if you don't care."

I'm speechless. Then, she smiles, leans in close to me, and says *(speaking as Rene)*:

"I might not be the smartest person in the room, but at least I know how to shut the fuck up."

I think I might be in love. Rene asks to join me. I tell her *"that would be great!"* And we both grab our things, pile them on top of our heads, make a beeline for the door, and just like that... this shitty job is done.

Now that I'm unemployed, I think it's time to move out of town. I'm diggin' the sound of New York City, and if I start walking now, I should get there in six to eight months. Have a nice voyage!

(Blackout. Holiday music plays. The screen projects a spiral galaxy as stars are projected all over the stage. Exit Al.)

Scene 3

(Enter Sonia, wearing a Christmas-themed uniform that includes a Santa hat and a red smock. There are holiday decorations and a fully-lit Christmas tree on stage. Lights up. Stars and music fade out.)

Sonia: Hi...

(She becomes irritated when the audience doesn't say "hi" back to her. She repeats herself.)

HI! *(she rolls her eyes)* My name is Sonia. My friends call me "Cookie," but for now, all of youse can just call me "Scrooge," okay? Call me that until the holiday season at the Cosmos Coffee Cup goes up in smoke, like the tacky-ass Yule log burning in the tacky-ass fireplace in your tacky-ass home, with all of its tacky-ass fucking stockings hanging from it!

I work at The Cup on 34th Street in Apple City. At Christmas time, it's known as "the miracle store," and it's a "miracle" that I haven't fucking killed anyone yet. I don't do anything in life besides work here, so stop asking! And in my free time, I do what I do, and *that* is ALL you need to know, is that clear?... Sorry if I come across a smidge cranky, but it's just that I FUCKING HATE CHRISTMAS! I think this time of year is total bullshit, and everything about it disgusts me, because everything about it is a lie.

Christmas time has nothing to do with Jesus Christ. Who the fuck was he again? It's not a time to celebrate "peace on Earth" or "good will towards men," or joy, or wishing, or any other bullshit Uncle Cosmo tries to shove up your ass, while he's in his cozy, quiet office, sipping on coffee, and meditating. No. Make no mistake about it. Christmas time is all about money and things. Spending money, buying things. Taking money, taking things. The only thing I ever hear this time of year is *"gimme, gimme, gimme, gimme, gimme,"* so why don't we just call Christmas the fucking *"Gimme Festival."* And... call me crazy, but it's kind of hard to get into the Christmas spirit around here when it's... November fucking 2nd! Halloween just fucking ended. What the fuck happened to Thanksgiving? Gobble gobble, anyone? Anyone? Fuck no! Gimme gimme. Turkey don't make no money, so now... it's time for Christmas. Time for greedy, bloodsucking corporations to abuse and overwork their employees, and time for every lonely, depressed, stressed-out, angry, dumb troll in the city to take out the pathetic states of their lives on me, and then self-medicate through shoving pig piles of slop into their bottomless pie holes.

Ya know, it's funny... because I thought customers were a little short with me before this "cheery" time of year. My panties would get all in a twist because people wouldn't pay attention to what I was saying, and it would really chap my ass when a customer, like the one standing over there, who's never worked a fucking day at my job, would try to tell me what to do, like he knew how my job worked, even though it's obvious, from the way that he's talking, that he has no fucking clue what he's talking about! I thought people were such a pain in the ass *before* Christmas? HAHAHAHA!!! I needed to shut the fuck up! I might as well have been on a God-damned vacation before, because Christmas customers are fucking DEMONS! Straight from hell. They are some of the most evil people you will ever come across on the face of the Earth. They find joy in torturing you, and they will do it as much as they can. I have never been more abused than I have at "the most wonderful time of the year."

Last Christmas, I messed up a customer's order. It was a *Supernova Eggnoggy Way Latte* with a complementary *Cosmos Coffee Cup Celestial Christmas Cookie,* and he screamed *"go to Hell"* at me... *(speaking as the customer)*:

"Go to Hell!!!!"

Really? Over a coffee and a free cookie? You wish me eternal damnation over a fucking coffee and a free cookie?! Ya know, it's too bad Jesus is nowhere to be found at The Cup during Christmas time, because some of you motherfuckers need him!

(Lights fade. Music plays. Lights up on Sonia, now standing at the Command Center.)

Sonia: Today is Wednesday. Another pain-in-the-ass kind of day, as is the norm during the Gimme Festival. It's the last half hour of my shift. The classic 8 to 4:30. A shift that only the best captains can work because you have to handle the *"double meteor shower:"* breakfast and lunch. It has been a hellish day, and things are only just now slowing down at 4:00 p.m. as opposed to the usual time of 2:30.

I'm holding things down at the Command Center, as usual, our store is a little messy after the rush, as usual, so my co-captains and I are resetting by cleaning and restocking everything, as usual, so our little Cup once again looks like the shiny fucking *jewel-in-a-space-age-crown it is*, as usual.

While we're tidying up, our store's decompression chamber opens, and in comes this lady with a real sour puss on her face. I can smell the stench of her rotten-ass attitude from across the store, and I know I hate this woman already.

I say *"Welcome to The Cup! How can I help you blast off?"*

She responds with *(speaking as customer)*:

"(snapping her fingers) I'm in a rush so can we speed this up?"

She's in a rush. *She* is in a *rush*. Stop everything! SHE is IN a RUSH, and *she* wants me to know that, because when a customer is in a rush, it is, of course, *my* fault, right?

She's trying me, but I have to be nice. I say *"Suuuuuuuuuuuuuuuuuuuuuuuuuuuuuure,"* nice and slow, petty as fuck. She snappily says *(speaking as customer)*:

"I'm double parked and I don't want to get a ticket."

Well, *that* changes everything! Now I feel compelled, with every fiber of my being, to get moving as fast as I can. She has double parked her car and, if I remember correctly, page 228 of the *Cosmo's Coffee Cup Captain's Manual* explicitly states that when a customer double parks her car, and puts herself at risk of getting a ticket while she goes into a store to WAIT in a line that's 5 miles long,... it's the *captain's* fault!

And, if I'm not mistaken, page 229 states that all captains are supposed to psychically attune themselves to the customer's whereabouts at all times in order to reserve parking spaces, and avoid any potential ticket risks. Why didn't I remember that?... Oh!... Right!... Because, on our planet, planet *Earth*, we're responsible for our *own* lives, so she can just try kissing my ass instead. But, since I can't say that to her face, I just say *"Okay, miss. What can I get for you?"*

She barks *(speaking as customer)*:

"A small coffee. Pour me whatever's fresh. I want it black, with two sugars, and I do not want to repeat myself."

I smile and nod, but I want to slap her. She don't know that, even while at work, these hands are rated E for Everyone.

Thankfully, my co-captain, Ricky, comes over to help me deal with this hag. We captains try to help one another as much as possible at The Cup, so our lovely customers can get their orders as quickly as possible, and then go crawl back under the bridges from which they came.

They say, *"What do you need, Sonia?"* I say *"A Giant coffee."* And this piece of work barks *(speaking as customer)*:

"Small! Small! I said SMALL!!!"

36

Oh, here we fucking go. Not only is she rude, she's never been to a God damned Cosmos Coffee Cup before... so with a force that damn near breaks my index finger, I point to the ENORMOUS FUCKING MENU BEHIND ME, and sweetly, slooooowly say *"Ma'am... a Giant IS a small."*

And she should have just said *"Okay..."*

...But instead, *Jackie Frost* over here has the nerve to say *(speaking as customer)*:

"Ugh! Whatever! This whole thing is just so confusing!"

So Ricky pours the GIANT small coffee for my frosty lil' customer and places it gingerly on the counter, eager as I am to get this asshole out of here ASAP. I tell her that her total is one dollar and fifty cents... and this partridge in a pear tree hands me a hundred-dollar bill. Who the FUCK orders a one- dollar-fifty-cent cup of coffee, and pays with a hundred -dollar bill?!

We can't break bills larger than twenty dollars at any Cosmos Coffee Cup because we're simply too busy and never, at any given time, have enough change in our cash craters. If this lady had ever stepped foot inside The Cup before, she would know that. But since this store is probably her first stop after getting out of Hell, or her last stop before going back, I have the responsibility of breaking the bad news.

I say, *"Sorry, Miss. We can't break that. Do you have anything smaller?"*

She says *(speaking as customer)*:

"No, I don't have anything smaller. That's money and I should be able to pay with it!"

I try to remain calm, even though I can feel my blood BOILING, and say *"I'm sorry, Miss. I don't have change for anything larger than a twenty. Do you have a credit card?"*

The hag says *(speaking as customer)*:

"Why don't you have change? I need change!"

So, I says to the hag, *"We don't have change because we're not a bank. There is a bank across the street if you need change, ma'am. Do you have a credit card?"*

She cuts me the look of death, then starts digging through her purse, saying *(speaking as customer)*:

"Fine. Fine! I don't have time for this. A woman should be

able to buy a cup of coffee without it being such a hassle. This
coffee is overpriced anyways. ."

And then... it happens. She pulls out her credit card, and
throws it at me!

Was it a toss? Did it just fly out of her hands on accident?
No. The wench threw it at me, all because I couldn't break
her hundred-dollar bill.

The credit card flies towards me at about 30 miles per hour
and hits me on the cheek, making a clapping sound on my
face. It hurts, and I'm pretty sure a Mastercard symbol is
imprinted on my cheek from a credit card that just bitch
-slapped me.

(Sonia becomes quiet) I need you all to know something
about me,... I grew up in a violent home, okay? You could
say that English was the second language in my home, and
violence was the first. The shit I seen and gone through is
the stuff from horror stories. I've had pieces of me broken,
inside and out. I grew up with nothing. No childhood, no
Christmas, nothing. I remember writing a letter to Santa
when I was seven years old, asking him to take me with him
to live in the North Pole for good. My father found the note,
and in the spirit of Christmas, decided to make me look like
Rudolph the Red-Nosed Reindeer. Just a normal day at

home. Every night, before bed, I used to pray to God to just kill me in my sleep, but they wouldn't do it, so I stopped believing in them. And then, on my twelfth birthday, I woke up to find out my parents had been killed in a car accident, and I reconsidered my faith. I know. I shouldn't find joy in someone's death, but it was the happiest day of my life, so it doesn't take a Rhodes scholar to figure out that I don't respond well to violence. *(Sonia grows increasingly angry)* So, when this *animal* threw her credit card at me... it was like I became a kid again, standing in my childhood home... powerless. I felt my throat close up, I couldn't breathe, I felt my hands becoming fists, my eyes glazed over, and I had a vision of myself taking this molten hot cup of coffee, throwing it right at her face, and hearing her scream *"AHHHHHH!"* That would have been the sweetest fucking Christmas carol ever sung!

(Blackout. Holiday music plays. Lights up. Music fades.)

Sonia: I think I blacked out for about 90 seconds. So when I come to and find myself back inside The Cup, I'm relieved to see everything looking just the way I left it, including... *(Sonia's eyes fixate back on the customer)* her, still staring me in the face. I've never been more thrilled to see something so butt-ass ugly in my life because it means I didn't beat her nasty lil' stank-faced ass to death.

I find myself just looking at this woman deep in her eyes, and that's when I see it. I know that look so well. It's kind of like a deer in headlights, or a feral cat, with a little bit of... I dunno... sadness mixed in. I could see in her eyes... that somewhere along her miserable trip to the present moment, someone made her feel powerless too.

I'm actually starting to feel sorry for this woman because I know how horrible this time of year is for people like us. I get her, and now I just want to do something to let her know she's going to be all right, you feel me? I want her to know that she isn't powerless and this bullshit time of year will be over soon enough. I smile at her, feeling damn proud of my newfound wisdom, but I must have failed. I must have looked like a feral cat, too, because this broad opens her mouth and says... *(speaking as customer)*:

"Gimme my fucking credit card"

(Sonia pauses for a moment)

Lemme tell you something about God. I consider myself a spiritual skeptic at this point, but the fact that my hands have somehow managed to refrain from wrapping themselves around her fucking neck to choke the miserable life out of her makes a strooooooooooooooooooooooong argument for their existence!

41

I take a deep breath, force myself to smile, and say (*slowly, through clenched teeth*) *"I just need to swipe your credit card, and then you'll be all set."*

So, I swipe the card, and something catches my eye. It's my Captain's Badge *(she points to the badge on her smock)*. It's a pin that displays your name, store number, and how many years you've worked for The Cup. I must have taken it off on my lunch break and forgot to put it back on. So, I see my badge on the counter, with its sharp pin tip sticking up... and as I'm handing *Her Royal Highness, The Snow Queen* her credit card with my right hand, I grab my badge with my left. I ask the *Ho Ho Ho* if she wants her receipt. She says *(speaking as customer)*:

"No. Just *gimme* my coffee."

I say *"Okay Ma'am,"* with an extra amount of holiday pep, grab her cup of coffee with both hands, and as I pick it up, I push my badge into her cup and poke a hole in it! I then pull the badge out, and hand her leaky cup to her at an angle so she can't tell the liquid is slooooooowly dripping out. *(Sonia looks to both sides)* No one saw what I just did, not even my co-captains!

Miss thing yanks her coffee out of my hands, damn near crushing her cup with her grip, and runs out of the store, leaving a tiny trail of coffee stretching out the door. By the time that Wintery Witch gets back on her broomstick, I know her cup will be empty, *(under her breath, still looking at the customer leaving the store, smiling as she speaks)* happy holidays, bitch.

(Lights fade. Music plays. Lights up on Sonia, now in the Captain's Quarters.)

Sonia: It's 4:30 now. Time to go home. I feel so fucking good that it's weirding me out. I mean I'm *never* like this at Christmas time. I think I'm starting to get why people start celebrating in November! It's almost as if my evil lil' customer performed some type of exorcism, sucking the crabbiness right outta me when she left. Or maybe I caught the Christmas spirit upon seeing her holy, and I do mean *hole*-y, grail.

I've decided to unwind in CQ for a bit before taking off. I've got me a *Giant Hot Chocolate Chondrite*, and I'm just gonna enjoy the shit outta this plush-ass chair.

One of my sweet co-captains, Shelly, left a spread of homemade Christmas cookies for us on the coffee table, still warm and in all these different types of holiday shapes. Looky here: we got trees, snowflakes, elves, Santas, and Grinches.

I'm looking at this Grinch cookie, bright green face all twisted and shit, red eyeballs bulging out of his head *(she laughs)* and I can't help but laugh because he looks so mean. *(she speaks to the cookie)* "Who pissed in your cuppa coffee?" *(she stops laughing)* But the more I'm staring at him, the more I start to see my customer,... then me,... and it hits me.

The Grinch is us. Hijacking Christmas to escape our own powerlessness, burying our joy in BS, like shitty little presents wrapped in ugly-ass boxes, and I gotta tell ya... I don't want to be like that anymore. Hell no. I want to be a pretty present with a fucking bow around it! And maybe Christmas is what it is to me... because I make it that way. So this year, while I'm feeling so damn good, maybe I'll try to love Christmas... or like it... or how about I hate it just a little bit less? I think I can do that. And let's be real. Not *everything* sucks about Christmas time. There are a lot of happy people around who do good things for others, like when Ricky held the door open for that hag when she flew outta my store, that was a *very good thing*... *(Christmas music starts to play in the background)* and the music we play at The Cup isn't so bad after all... and the *Eggnoggy Way Latte* we serve this time of year is pretty fucking tasty, if Eggnog is your kinda thing... and that motherfucker in the red suit... has always been kinda cute... holy shit! I feel jolly.

This is a fucking trip, but I think I like the way jolly feels. So from here on out, I promise that the only heads I'll be biting off during Christmas time will be the ones on holiday cookies (*she takes a bite out of the Grinch cookie, continuing to speak while chewing*). And to all of you, I just want to say, even though it's November 2nd... Merry fucking Christmas. Have a nice voyage this season.

(Blackout. Holiday music plays. The screen projects a starry night with a full moon, across which the silhouette of Santa in his sleigh, being pulled by his reindeer, flies by. Exit Sonia. Music fades out. End of Act One.)

Act Two

Scene 1

(Enter Bijoux. Lights up. Stars and music fade out.)

Bijoux: *Salut.* My name is Bijoux. You can call me 'B' for
short. I work at The Cup on Walnut Street in San Cristóbal.
I am originally from Haiti. From a place called Milot. Have
you heard of it? I'm forty years old, and I moved to the
United States from Canada two years and seven months ago.
I was a doctor in Haiti, and in Canada, but I am not yet able
to practice medicine in the United States, though I plan to
in the future.

About a year and a half ago, my wife, who is also from
Canada, became very ill. I think America made her sick.
I'm kidding. But all joking aside, it has been very difficult to
watch such a strong, joyous woman become so weak and
frail, so far from our families in Canada and Haiti. She has
decent health insurance from her job, which is what
brought us to the States from Canada, but with healthcare
being so very expensive here, we had to do something to
help with the costs of her treatment. So now, I am working
for The Cup because it has great medical benefits. This job
is a blessing, and I am very grateful for it. My wife's
condition is improving every day, and with the added
insurance from my job, we are able to manage the costs.

Life is not easy, but we are surviving. We take each day as it comes, and today is a good day. My wife is able to get the treatment she needs. That is all I really care about. And I am perfectly fine at my job for the time being. In fact, I really enjoy working at The Cup. I think it is a marvelous company! There's always something new and exciting to learn each day, and I absolutely love the people I work with, but I must say... some of you customers need to... how do you say it?... "Get out more?" See the world outside your bubble, yes? What do you know about other places in the world? About Haiti? And what do you know about me apart from what I've only just told you? If you answered "nothing" to any of my questions, I suggest you try to find an answer before you come to a conclusion on the matter.

Working at The Cup, I am often frightened by how many people I see each day who don't care to find the answer to a question, or who simply accept information that is incorrect *as* the answer. I believe that is how ignorance is born. One must always try to find the answer to a question, and then question the answer when one finds it to be sure the information is correct. And then, over time, one must question the answer again because the answer might change, and that is why I love medicine. Medicine teaches me to always look for new answers to our questions, and seek out new and exciting ways to make life better. That, to me, is what living in the States is all about, making life better.

50

I am fascinated by the States. I think it is a beautiful place, and I am learning much about the States through serving food and drink. This truly is the land of plenty. There are so many choices here, so much variety, but I often wonder if it is... too much? Not because of the choices, I am a big fan of the right to choose, believe me, but... I wonder if there are too many choices because of how much goes to waste.

Take where I work for example. My store is part of a larger complex that houses not only our store, but also a bakery, a clothing store, and a store that sells things for the home. We place all of our garbage in two dumpsters located directly behind the complex. No dumpster is assigned to any particular store, but the garbage from The Cup and the bakery tend to go in the dumpster on the left, and the garbage from the clothing store and the goodies-for-the-home store tend to go in the dumpster on the right.

On any given day, one can find fresh food, new clothing, art, dishes, even chairs and stools, all wrapped in plastic, in the dumpsters. Practically new, practically fresh, and when I tell you that the food is still good, I mean it. One does not have to be a doctor to be able to tell when food is perfectly good to eat. It looks as if it just came out of the oven, and went straight into the trash... wasted.

See these shoes I am wearing? I found them new, inside the

box, wrapped in plastic, in the dumpster on the right. The original price tag was still on them. They were two hundred dollars. Brand new, two-hundred-dollar shoes in the garbage. I found them along with ten dress shirts, and eight pairs of pants, and this is not unusual at all. Actually, this is quite typical of the dumpster on the right. Come to think of it, the only "garbage" one ever sees in the dumpster on the right is paper, so I guess the people who own the complex have never heard of recycling... nor do they care to.

We don't recycle at The Cup either. This frightens me because ninety percent of our products are served on, or stored in paper, plastic, and glass. How hard is it to get a recycling bin? Surely we can do better.

I donated the shirts and pants I found to my local thrift store. At the drop-off, I kept hearing a loud, crashing sound coming from the section where the dishes were kept. Upon closer inspection, I found an employee throwing dishes into a garbage can as if they were baseballs. Crash. Crash. Crash. It was so loud. I asked them why they were throwing perfectly good dishes into the garbage. *They told me (speaking as employee)*:

"That's where they go when there isn't enough room for them."

So, I said *"Let me take them, please! I will find someone who can use them."*

And they said *(speaking as employee)*:

"Sorry, I can't do that. Store policy."

STORE POLICY?!? Perfectly good plates, bowls, and cups, now in pieces because of store policy? Surely we can do better.

That is why I try, as often as I can, to grab a bag or two from the many "dumpsters on the right" in my town, and do something with what I find. One cannot let perfectly good things go to waste. Even if you take just one thing from one dumpster, someone somewhere needs it.

When I see such waste, I wonder if things are really as bad as people say they are here in the States. I know things are not great. I see many people who are going without, but... I have yet to see an empty grocery store... I have yet to see a car dealership around here with no cars, I have yet to see any people move into the empty houses on my street *and* the next street over... and I have yet to see *actual* garbage in the dumpster on the right,... so this still looks like the "land of plenty" to me. I wonder if there really is a problem, or is the answer simply not good enough?

I am also intrigued by the idea of what it means to be an American. To be seen as American, and it amazes me what people will do to prove their love for this country. I have seen more than a few people dismiss people who look like them, because of the way they act, or talk, all for the sake of being seen as American.

By the way, in case you haven't noticed, I have an accent. It's true. I have been told that it is rather lovely, and I'd have to agree. That was actually the first thing my wife said to me.

I was at a subway station. I was talking on the phone. I hate talking on the phone in public places, but it was an important call, and thank goodness it was brief, because when I hung up, she came up to me and said *"You have a lovely accent."* She also said that I was *"drop-dead gorgeous (Bijoux giggles)."* Normally, I don't respond to flattery, but... there was something peculiar about her, and the way she looked at me... I felt a glow coming from her. It was almost... holy, as strange as that might sound. I felt as if I knew her already, and I felt safe around her, so I introduced myself to her, and did not put my phone back into my bag until I had her phone number within it.

My wife has an accent too. It is very musical, but she is from Canada, and not the French-speaking part, so no one around here seems to care. No, it is my accent that tends to make people uncomfortable. Why? What is so scary about someone who is from somewhere else? Do you think I won't understand you? I ask that question, because every day I get a customer who feels a need to talk to me like I am stupid. At first, I thought it was because I was new, but I have worked here for a year now, and many customers still do it. Or, they'll make a point of telling me how much change to give back to them when they pay for their orders, right down to the type of coin, as if I cannot add... and then, they become defensive when I correct them because they did not properly do the math.

Some customers feel they must speak slowly to me, so now I've just made a point of doing it back to them:

"Aaaannnnnn-yyyyy-thinggg el-ssssse foooorrr yooooooou?..."

Some people will mumble their orders and become irritated when I ask them to repeat themselves, as If I don't understand English. Wrong answer. The real problem is that *you* were not speaking English, so I could not understand you. Speak English, and we'll get somewhere. I promise you, no matter how complex your order, I am up for the challenge. I was a doctor in Haiti. A doctor! If I can diagnose rare forms of cancer, then I am pretty sure I have the skills needed to pour a cup of coffee!

(Lights fade. Music plays. Lights up on Bijoux, now standing at the Command Center.)

Bijoux: I do not believe in doing something if I cannot do my best, so I always give one-hundred percent of myself to my job. In this store, I am known for my flawless work ethic, and for keeping The Cup clean. Just look around you. This store sparkles like a diamond. My co-captains call me "Captain Clean," "C.C," and "Double C *(Bijoux laughs)*." They even like to poke a little fun at me because I can be quite tough on dirt, but a store is like a hospital, and must be kept sanitary at all times.

I am most proud of the fact that my store is the only store in the country to receive two consecutive perfect scores during health inspections. Do you know how big of a deal that is?

Listen, I am not the commander of my store, I'm not even a supervising captain, but I know this store could not have done it without me, so I have no problems accepting full credit for it.

I remember the day we got our second perfect score as if it happened this morning. We almost didn't get it. You should have been there.

(Lights transition to a spotlight on Bijoux)

Today is Thursday. We are having one of the worst meteor showers I have ever seen in our store. There are customers everywhere. A sea of people yelling, eating, drinking, spilling, throwing their trash on the floor, causing crumbs and stains to fly everywhere. It is a mess! Never in my year at The Cup have I ever seen my store look like this. I want to scream, but a doctor must remain calm during an emergency... and then I hear it. The voice. I have not heard it since I was a practicing doctor, but it always tells me the right thing to do. This time, it says *"Grab the tool belt. You'll know what to do."* So, without question, I reach down into the cabinet under the sink, take it out, remove the tools, and replace them with spray bottles of surface cleaner, towels, and gloves. What a rush! I feel like I am back in the operating room... I've missed that feeling. I strap the toolbelt around my waist, put on my plastic gloves, and call over to our commander Jerry, through all of those people. I say *"Commander? Permission to abort the Command Center, stat, and clean?"*

And, Jerry says *(speaking as Jerry)*:

"No, Captain! It is too dangerous!"

But, I hold my ground and say *"Don't worry about me, Commander. I'll be fine."*

Jerry says *(speaking as Jerry)*:

"Roger. Command Center reinforcements have successfully been deployed. Good luck, Captain. Be safe!"

...and sends me on my way.

I start at the customer seating area. Tables wiped, chairs wiped, stains removed, crumbs eliminated, clear!

Then, I move around the perimeter of the store. Walls wiped, lights wiped and dusted, clear!

Next, I glide to the customer restrooms. We have a code brown in one of the stalls! I grab a mop, perform an emergency *soil-ectomy* on the floor, then clean and sanitize all surfaces! Clear!

And then, to finish, I grab my trusty broom once more, and sweep. I sweep with every fiber of my being! Weaving in and out of people, blasting the last bits of crumbs and dirt, sweeping up a storm!

The rest is a blur. I don't remember exactly what happened after that, but next thing I know, I am standing in the middle of a spotless store... just in time for the health inspector to arrive.

(Lights transition back to normal)

He makes his inspections as usual and seems to be very impressed. *"How do you keep such a busy store so clean?"* he asks.

Jerry says to the inspector *(speaking as Jerry)*:

"Well, I have my secret weapons. There's our store supervising captain, Elizabeth..."

And Elizabeth waves to the inspector and says "Hello!"

The inspector walks over to her, shakes her hand, and says *(speaking as inspector)* *"Hello! Great work!"*

Then, Jerry says *(as Jerry)*:

"... And we have our resident captain of cleanliness, Bijoux."

I smile at the inspector, and say *"Hello,..."* and he just glares at me, turns back to Jerry, and says *(as inspector)*:

"Well, that's nice. I'd like to step into your office."

No "hello" for me, and no handshake.

Well, they were in the office for about five minutes, before the inspector comes out and says *"Great work, everyone!"* Then, he kind of glares at me again and leaves the store. A few seconds later, Jerry comes out of the office and yells *"We got a perfect score!"*

All of my co-captains are cheering and hugging, and I join in with them, but on the inside, I have a sour feeling. It is a feeling that I hate to allow myself to feel, but to deny it would cause even more discomfort. I feel... like I don't belong, and I want to leave, but then I think about my wife, how I've begun to see that glow again in the last week or so, and I remember why I am here. So, I take a deep breath, in *(they inhale)* and out *(they exhale)*, and compose myself.

That inspector had no reason to be unfriendly to me. I was introduced to him, after all, as the person responsible for keeping the store clean. He did not come across as shy or reserved, and he was perfectly friendly to Jerry, Elizabeth, and my co-captains, so there can only be one reason for this feeling: code *brown*.

Oh, I am not a sensitive person when it comes to these kinds of things. I do not take brown skin and an accent very seriously. This body, after all, is just a suit. It doesn't really mean anything. All the good stuff lies beneath it. And, as a doctor who has performed many surgeries, I must tell you that we are all quite the same on the inside. But, then again... I am smart. I am not satisfied with old answers to questions, so perhaps it is easier for me to see this than others.

I don't know where the health inspector came from, or what his life is like, but I shall not remain upset for long. He is, after all, a product of his environment, and, in my opinion, from my experiences in the States, very *un*-American. He is just one person, out of over three hundred thirty million people from the States, as I am just one of over twelve million people from Haiti. It would be foolish to dismiss an entire group of people just because of how he, one person, treated me. I don't know about you, but I have always believed that an open mind is the answer to a closed one.

Besides, my co-captains were so joyful that morning, I was not going to let a perfectly good day end up in the dumpster on the right. And I was not going to give any one person, customer or not, permission to make me feel like I don't belong. Wherever you choose to be, that is where you belong! And this is my home now. Here, in this fascinating place. I have so much to learn, so I intend to keep experiencing, and questioning... until I find the right answer for me. That is the best I can do. I wish you good questions and excellent health. Have a nice voyage. Doctor's orders!

(Blackout. Space-age music plays. The screen projects a spiral galaxy as stars are projected all over the stage. Exit Bijoux.)

Scene 2

(Enter Randy. Lights up. Stars and music fade out.)

Randy: Hey Y'all! I'm Randy. I work at The Cup in town center, right here in the heart of good ol' Green Valley. Green Valley is a cute little town. Adorable. I like to call Green Valley the place with small town charm, and big city problems. I grew up here, and I have worked at The Cup for six years. Around here, I am what's known as a "store training captain." That means I teach new captains everything about the Cosmos Coffee Cup including company history, products, policies and procedures. People like me to train 'em 'cause I don't let people make mistakes without tellin' 'em straight up that they messed up.

Now, I was raised right, so I'm never mean, but I *am* direct and honest 'cause that is how I like people to be with me, but who are we kiddin? Here in Green Valley, we prefer gossipin' over the direct approach... and people love to talk about me, 'cause around here... I am what's known as a "Sweet Tea." That ain't a name I came up with. I don't know who came up with it, but people 'round here like to use it whenever they want to describe anyone who's... "like that," another term they use, or "funny," another term they use. "Funny," which I don't find funny AT ALL. And I don't like "Sweet Tea" neither. Not even the real thing. Too much damn sugar! Now, I'll tolerate "like that," depending on the day I'm having and your tone of voice. If I hear any disrespect in your tone, I'ma ask you *"Like what?"*

And you better have the right answer or you're fixin' to get cussed out, and let me tell y'all, there's plenty of good cussin' in Green Valley!

Now, Green Valley ain't a big place, but it is bigger than Peachville. Let me tell y'all about Peachville!

Peachville ain't even technically a town. Hell, I don't even know what you call it. All I know is it's real small. Ain't much more than a bunch of houses there, but it's real pretty, and it's a great time. It's located about an hour outside of Green Valley, and you don't travel there unless you got a reason to. It's hard to find 'cause it's not on the maps, and you take dirt roads to get there.

You'll know you've reached Peachville when you see the gate. There's a big ol' gate 'round the whole village, and you find a place to park in the big open clearin' right outside the gate. Next, you gotta call someone who lives in Peachville year round to let you in, and if you don't know someone you can call to let you in, you better be with someone who knows someone you can call to let you in, or y'all ain't gettin' in. Once you're in, you're home, you're free, and you can visit any of the various houses there for your needs. Need medication for your "sinner's disease" 'cause your doctor back home won't treat you? Go to the light green house. Wanna dance in leather? Go to the light blue house. Lace? Go to the red house. What else?... Wanna speak to a psychic? Go to the dark green house, and if you want to sit down and have a nice bite to eat, go to the white house. There are other houses, too, for all different kinds of needs... but I can't tell y'all about those. Y'all will have to go there to see them with your own eyes... if y'all are "like that."

Now, there are two married men from Green Valley who frequent Peachville: Amos Carver, and Maxwell DuBois. I went to high school with Amos and Max. They were both very popular, and they each married one of the two purdiest gals in Green Valley: Mindy and Cindy. Best friends, and two of the biggest brats I have ever met! Now, Amos and Max don't cause me no trouble 'cause they don't wanna be exposed, but Mindy and Cindy love to make me suffer. They do it 'cause they hate all things "sweet tea." Well, that and... I kissed Amos in high school. I didn't tell anyone. It wasn't that great anyway. His mouth tasted like deviled eggs. EEEEEE-YUCK!

I kissed Max, too. It was *delicious*, and Cindy walked in on it! To this day, I think that's how she pressured Max into marrying her. See, Max had an image to uphold. He's "the pride and joy of Green Valley." He was our high school valedictorian, captain of the wrestling team, he rescued a kitten from a burning building, went to Harvard Law School, and now he's in the family business, running a very successful law firm in Green Valley's business district. I'm pretty sure he shits fourteen karat gold nuggets, too!

People would DIE if they knew the pride and joy was a "sweet tea." The "Honorable Mayor of Green Valley" cannot have an only son who is "like that!" It would probably kill him. Cindy knows that, and she uses it to her advantage every chance she can get, and Mindy copies everything Cindy does, just like she did back in high school, 'cause, bless her lil' ol' heart, she's never been good at thinking.

Every day, those two brats come inside The Cup and try to do something that'll get me sent home for the day. It never works, and I usually just let whatever they say roll off my back anyhow, but something happened two months ago that I couldn't let slide.

(Lights fade. Music plays. Lights up on Randy, now standing at the Command Center.)

Randy: Today is Friday. We just had our morning meteor

shower, and things could best be described as "uneventful." Like clockwork, the two brats, and their husbands, have come into my store for a "lil' snack" after their morning jog, and right away, they're starting their shit with me.

Today, the brats have decided it's *Lets Take Our Sweet-Ass Time Orderin' Even Though There's a Line of Customers in the Store Day.* So, I take it upon myself to tell the brats to hurry up because other customers are waiting, and that's when Mindy, in full Karen mode, tells me to *(as Mindy)*:

"Let 'em wait! It's our turn! Where are your manners? Let me speak to your commander!"

And then, Cindy chimes in and says *(as Cindy)*:

"I blame your mother! What God-loving woman would let her son turn out like THAT?"

I told y'all we all went to high school together, so these two brats know damn well that my momma is dead. She passed away when I was eighteen. A rare blood disorder took her from this world. She needed a blood donor. She had a rare blood-type. I was a perfect match, but since Green Valley is a small town, it was pretty much common knowledge that I was "like that," and when you're "like that," the hospitals 'round here won't take your "funny" blood. So, I couldn't

67

save her. *(He pauses for a moment)* They even made me sign a form swearing to never give blood to anyone, ever.

What the hell is wrong with people? I'm perfectly healthy, I don't have any diseases, and I take great care of myself! What was my blood gonna do to her? Make her love men even more? I wish she woulda' lived so we coulda' found out.

My momma. The only woman I ever loved. She used to tell me *(speaking as his momma)*:

"Baby, God made you like that. So, if you need to cuss somebody out when they try to tell you somethin' different, know that you have his blessing."

And that is why I can cuss the way I can. 'Cause when I'm cussin' someone out, I'm doin' it for my momma and God!

Now, there are certain things you just shouldn't bring up, no matter what you think of a person. I might hate Cindy and Mindy, but I would never bring up something like that, ever! I knew I had to do something, and it had to be something that wouldn't get me fired, so I leave the floor and tell my commander what happened. He asks me if I'm all right, then tells me to take ten minutes to get myself together, he would step in and finish with Cindy, Mindy, and the rest of the customers.

I go outside to get me some fresh air, telling myself, "Come on, Randy! Think. Think!!!!" Ah-ha! And like magic, I picture *Travis*, my best friend. Travis is the most popular hairdresser in Green Valley. His salon, *Southern Belle*, is right around the corner from The Cup. He does all things hair and makeup, for all skin tones and hair textures, and he does not miss! He don't really talk about it, but he's "like that" too, and cannot stand Cindy 'cause of the way she treats me and the other sweet teas. He only does her hair 'cause she knows everyone in this town, and he makes her hair look so damn good that it brings in a lot of business for him. I guess some people will put aside their differences in the name of hair. That, and Cindy is a steady paycheck... 'cause she's got a full head of gray hair that must always be kept hidden. Travis makes her blonde, and he does such a fabulous job that even I have to admit. . she is, without a doubt, one of the purdiest *Golden Retrievers* I ever saw! She gets her hair done every second Friday right after terrorizing me, so I knew she would be heading to Southern Belle today!

So, I call Travis, and tell him what happened. He ain't sayin' nothin', but there's this thing he does when he's real fired up. He breathes heavy and loud through his nose, like a bull, and that's how you know... ooh-wee! Someone's in trouble! All I hear is *(he makes loud breathing sound three times)*... so I say *"Travis? Are you okay?..."*

69

He says *(speaking as Travis)*:

"Mmmhmmm (he makes another loud breathing sound),"

...then hangs up.

I can't call him back 'cause my break is over. So, I just go back to work as normal, knowing the brats are well on their way to Southern Belle, without the slightest clue what Travis is going to do.

Well, the remaining three hours of my shift fly by smoother than anything. Then, just as I'm about to clock out for the day, there is a commotion at the decompression chamber, and in comes Cindy, still wearing her Southern Belle smock, and sporting gorgeous, feathered, flipped, and *neon-violet -colored* hair *(he laughs)*!

I'm telling y'all, it looked like an electric-purple Christmas tree! Her hair is stiff as a board, and does not budge, no matter how badly she's shaking with anger. Everyone in the store freezes, then bursts out laughing. People are hunched over, crying, and pointing... I'm laughing right along with 'em, and that's when she pushes me then screams *(speaking as Cindy)*:

"I know you're behind this you evil little FAGGOT!!!"

Of course, the laughter stops, and I'm just standing there, not saying a word... when all of sudden I hear my momma's voice, loud and clear, say... *"GET 'ER!"*

(A spotlight appears on Randy)

So, I lean in real close to Miss Cindy and say:

"Listen, sweetie, and listen carefully, 'cause I'm only gonna tell you once. Unless you want some black and blue to go with that purple hair, you better just shut your ugly ass on up! Now, I'm gonna call Travis, and he's gonna fix this, but don't you start any more of your shit with me or anyone else EVER again, 'cause us faggots, we stick together, and we're everywhere in this town, and we're all waiting to turn Green Valley into the hell you belong in! I know you got your cousin's wedding to go to pretty soon. You tried on your dress yet? How'd you like to look like a stuffed sausage? I'm sure your husband would enjoy it 'cause he sure does LOVE sausage."

She looks at me, trembling, with tears in her eyes, and says *(speaking as Cindy)*:

"All right! Call him."

(Lights return to normal)

71

Like I said, some people will put aside their differences in the name of hair.

I call Travis. Cindy goes back to Southern Belle and gets her hair fixed. It turned out the purple color was only temporary, and the world's most beautiful Golden Retriever was able to go to the wedding and catch the bouquet in her mouth. Good girl! And she never bothered me again *(he snaps his fingers)*.

Come to think of it, I ain't really had to cuss nobody out since I read the dog shit outta Cindy. I think Green Valley changed a little that day, 'cause now people ain't really hiding no more.

Every day, I get more and more people who are "like that" coming into my store. Today, one of us came up to me and said *"Thank you for teaching that asshole a lesson! We're tired of hiding. We're part of Green Valley too!"*

There's even talk of opening a bar here in town center for people who are "like that." It might be trouble, but we ain't afraid. Besides, we got a few folks in the police department who are "like that" too, so who knows? Maybe, in time, Peachville will just be a summer vacation spot. Now, we got a long way to go here in Green Valley, but it has *never* looked better. Life is sweet when you don't hide, and when you don't take any sheeyit! I do hope y'all will come back 'round here real soon! But until then, keep on cussin' out fear in the name of love. And remember to have a nice voyage.

(Blackout. Space-age music plays. The screen projects a spiral galaxy as stars are projected all over the stage. Exit Randy.)

Scene 3

(Enter Sage. Lights up. Stars and music fade out.)

Sage: Peace and blessings. My name is Sage. Just Sage, and I have shared much of the last seven years of my time with my family at The Cup on Cedar Lane, in Great Falls. I love my home on Cedar Lane. It truly is the most beautiful store. It sits on top of a large hill, and gives you spectacular views of the city, the Purple Mountains, and Great Falls, the tallest waterfall in the region. In fact, if we all were to become silent for a moment, you'd be able to hear Great Falls sing. Let's try it! Shhhh... ahhh, do you hear it? It's magic, and when I come into work each morning, and I climb that hill... with the sunlight and fresh air kissing my face, the Cedar trees greeting me, and Great Falls singing her song to me... I can feel my soul ascending. I can hear Mother Earth saying *"Good morning, my child. I love you,"* and I take that love, wrap it around my spiritual vessel, feel it radiating through the energetic channels of my body, and I am ready for the day. And when I see my home, I start to run towards it because I can't wait to see my beautiful siblings, and when I enter the Fifth Dimension, my siblings greet me with expressions of joy, gratitude, appreciation... and I am home. Welcome home. I love my home. My heart dances.

When I am home, all the problems of the world become this big *(Sage pinches their fingers together)*. When I am home, there is no war, no disease, no poverty, and all that matters is enjoying life, feeding the community, and making the world a better place, one cup at a time. That is what life is all about, and for seven years, I have freely given my life to my home to honor that mission. That is... until today.

Today, my store commander, or our *store father*, as we call him, brought me into the Captain's Quarters, and said *"Sage... I am sorry, my child, but you must leave our home."*

I said *"Why, Father? What did I do? Why must I leave home?"* And, that was when he told me...

I close our home every Friday evening with my sister, Willow, and my brother, Jasper. We almost always have cuisine of which we must dispose because it will expire over the weekend, when our home is closed. We are able to donate the leftover pastries to a shelter for battered women, downtown, but The Cup has a strict policy stating that we have to dispose of the rest because of company liability, say if someone were to become ill after eating them. I understand the company has rules to follow, and a reputation to protect, but none of the "rule-makers" work in our homes, and none of them have ever had the honor of meeting Robert.

Robert is *beautiful*. He is somewhere over 70 years old, with ice-blue eyes, alabaster hair that he keeps in a clean crew cut, and a laugh that could make a stone smile. He walks with a cane that he carved himself out of Vietnamese golden cypress, and you feel as if winter has just ended whenever he is near. I call him "Pops" because he reminds me so much of my grandfather.

Pops tells the best stories. My favorite ones are about his childhood in San Francisco, and his time in the circus as a lion tamer. The harder stories to hear are about his time in the war, and his life since coming back home.

Pops has the most beautiful smile. You don't see that kind of smile very often. It's the kind that glows from the inside, and I don't care what kind of day you're having, just have Pops smile at you, and your day will turn around. I once asked Pops why he smiled so much, and he said *(speaking as Pops)*:

"Why not? You always have a choice. Choose something that'll make you smile. Just look at all these sour pusses running around. We got enough of 'em, don't you think?"

Pops lives, part-time, at the disabled veteran's shelter just north of here. Not every veteran can be housed at the same time, so everyone must follow some kind of rotating schedule for staying there. I have no idea where Pops goes when he's not staying at the shelter, but I do know that I love him, and although I do not believe in war, I respect him because deep down in our hearts, we both want the same thing: to serve humanity, and make the world a better place, and it is so rare to meet someone who would give his life for a cause, I just felt compelled to do something for him every time I saw him.

So, on a random Friday evening, years ago, just before we were about to close our home for the weekend, Pops came in and asked if we had any sandwiches that we were going to throw out because the boys at the shelter were hungry, and they were going to draw straws to see which one of them would be eaten for the night *(Sage laughs)*. I said *"Sure, Pops,"* put the sandwiches in a large bag, and handed them to him. He gave me a salute, then went on his way, cane in one hand, and bag full of sandwiches in the other *(Sage waves as if they're watching Robert leave)*. After that, he would come in every Friday evening, just before we closed, I would put the sandwiches in a bag for him, and he'd take them and go. They were just going to go in the trash, and they were still good until Sunday... I figured it was the least I could do, considering his service *and* sacrifice to this country. Our home.

Pops lost three toes and leg tissue when his buddy stepped

on a land mine just two feet away from him. To this day, he still has shrapnel in both hips.

(Speaking as Pops) "Eh, it coulda been worse," he says. *"My buddy lost everything."*

...It was the least I could do. Just some old sandwiches... it was the least I could do...

...Well, that was one rule that I couldn't break and still expect to keep my home.

I used to pour him a cup of coffee too. One of my free daily drinks. That's not allowed either... so, I was asked to leave home. Seven years here, and I'm being kicked out of my home.

I feel pain, but I do not believe in mistakes. No. I believe in order in the Universe, so I know that the Cosmos, or God, or whatever you want to call it, is calling me to another place. I don't know where I will go, or what I will do, but I trust myself, and no matter what, I will always follow my heart.

Fortunately, I have always found it quite difficult to hold on to anger when Spring is here. Just look around. Everything is in bloom, the air is becoming warm and sweet, spreading the good news of birth and renewal; the Sun is shining at least ten times brighter than before, and Great Falls is singing! Shhhh. Just listen...

Today is Saturday. The time is now. So, before I say goodbye to you, I am going to buy a couple of sandwiches, and put them in a bag, because I hear an infectious laugh coming from just outside my home... and it is the least I can do.

Please don't worry about me, my loves. Nothing good ever came from worrying, and I'll be fine. Really. I am... at peace with what has happened... Yes.

I wish you many blessings on your life's journey. Choose something that will make you smile, and you *will* have a nice voyage.

(Blackout. Space-age music plays. The screen projects a spiral galaxy as stars are projected all over the stage. Exit Sage.)

Scene 4

(Enter Ronnie. Their location will change based on the location of the production of this play. Lights up. Stars and music fade out.)

Ronnie: Hello! I'm Ronnie. I work at The Cup on *(insert name of street)*, in *(insert name of city)*, and this is a very special day. Today marks my ninth anniversary at The Cup, may I have a round of applause for that? Thank you! And,... today is also my last day here! That's right. After being a faithful Cosmos Coffee Cup captain for the last nine years, I've decided I don't want to work here anymore, so I'm quitting. Allow me to explain why.

A year ago, when I passed the 8-year mark with this company, I felt like I had finally reached a point where there was nothing wrong with my job. I was happy until, out of nowhere, I started to find myself irritated by random little things that never bothered me before. A special request from a customer, a loud laugh in-store, and I couldn't shake the thought of punching my happy co-captains for no good reason.

I did my best to put on a game face, smile through it all, and be a cheery captain for everyone, but it was all an act.

Within weeks, I was completely miserable.

Then, on one random day, during one of the busiest morning meteor showers we've ever had in our store, it hit me. I looked around, at my happy co-captains, the countless customers in the store,... and what I saw was... nothing. Sure, we were moving around and doing things... but it all seemed pointless to me. In that hollow moment, I discovered what the problem was. Me. And it turned out I wasn't actually annoyed by anyone or anything in particular, just disappointed that no one else was able to feel what I was feeling.

I felt the urge to punch someone again, but this time that someone was me because it was selfish and foolish of me not to want my co-captains to be happy. They love where they work. Life is so much better when you love where you work... but who am I to talk? I have never, ever known the feeling.

I started working at The Cup because I needed a day job. Something to sustain me while I figured out my life. I never intended to work here this long, but sometimes you settle into a groove, one day bleeds into the next day, and that day spills over into the next day that melts into the next day, and before you know it, almost a decade has passed, and you're still doing the same thing. And that's fine, if you love it, but if you don't love it, it scares the shit out of you. I don't want to disrespect Uncle Cosmo, or any of the people who work for this company, because this is a *great* place to work, you know? And some people have said really disrespectful things to us captains, like *"What are you going to do for a real job?"* As if working here is a fake job...

Every job is a real job, okay? And this job has been a very real blessing. It has paid my bills, my rent, bought me things... but I don't love it. I want to do something else. I have vivid dreams...

I've never told anyone this before, but there are three things in my life that I love more than anything in the world: dancing, baking, and writing, and I've always dreamed of combining them in a really cool way that would bring people together.

I've got it all figured out. There's this two-story building for lease downtown. I pass by it every day on my way to work. It used to be an O.M.G. Thursdays. The first floor has a fully-functioning, industrial kitchen, the second floor has plenty of open space, and the whole building has really big windows, so I know it gets great light. It looks like the perfect building for my vision, so... I am making plans to lease that building, and open a bakery-bookstore-nightclub.

I'm going to call it *Good, Clean, Fun* because everything that will go on at my bakery-bookstore-nightclub will be good, clean, and fun. No chemicals, no additives, no drugs, no alcohol. I would only use organic, locally-grown ingredients in my baked goods, and I would make it possible for people to enjoy a sweet regardless of their dietary or financial restrictions.

To tie my bakery into my bookstore, I'd name my baked goods after famous novels and authors. I already have a recipe for a sweet roll made with honey and sea salt that I'm going to call a *"Seabiscuit."* Seabiscuit!!! My Seabiscuit is delicious with coffee, which we will also serve at *Good, Clean, Fun*, of course! I mean hey, why let a good skill go to waste?

In the bakery bookstore, I'll display my books and baked goods on the same types of shelving and glass cases so my books look just as mouth-wateringly delicious as my baked goods, like my *"Sweet Bar Named Desire;"* It's a blonde brownie.

At *Good, Clean, Fun,* I'd also be able to sell literature and art from local artists, and every customer would always get a free pastry with the purchase of any book. Everyone in the neighborhood would be welcome to sit in our fully wheelchair-accessible lounges, downstairs or upstairs, to read, eat, and use our free wifi.

Upstairs, in the open space, I'd have more tables and chairs set out for our customers, and the big windows would provide spectacular, territorial views of the city. I'd also have enough space to accommodate authors and guest speakers who would like to host talks, and I could hold community events and host open mic nights anytime the people want.

For my nightclub, we would move the tables and chairs along the walls, so people could sit if needed, and we'd keep everything very simple. Nothing elaborate. Just a nice, clean, open space, with killer lighting, and a platform for the DJ that could double as a stage for the bookstore's guest speakers.

The nightclub would be a place for people who just wanted to dance. Not drink, not drug, just dance. We would play grooves from different eras. Classics, unknown songs *(dance music starts to play, Ronnie starts to dance in a percussive style)*, new artists, you name it... and people from all over the world could come together and just dance. Vibrate with the sounds. You could speak a different language, you could have absolutely no money, you could be a terrible dancer, but as long as you had love and music in your heartbeat, you could just come on in... and dance. Let go! Be free! Let your senses merge with rhythm and melody.

With each beat, we'd become children again. Playing in a symphonic sandbox for the first time. Reborn to explore the grains and textures of each song, our shapes and colors simultaneously blurring into a living tapestry, expanding with the groove. The rhythm settles us into the zone, and we become an ocean. The molecules of us oscillate in sound waves of liquid tones. Ebbing and flowing, we rock and crash together. Kick. Jump. Spin. Dip. Can you feel it?

(The music changes to slow, ambient music. Lights dim. Ronnie's movements become slow and fluid.)

There would be no separation between the concept of "you" and "me," just perspiration from the bliss of personifying dance deep into the night. We'd shake it through the sky, bounce behind the stars, into a new dimension and beyond.

(Music fades out. Lights return to normal. Ronnie stops dancing.)

A wise man said *"Hold fast to dreams."*

Right now, it's only real in here *(points to head)*, and here *(points to heart)*, but I'll get it out here by putting my dreams out there. I know I can do it, because I'm allowing myself to... because I'm willing... and because I've stopped hiding inside The Cup. I really liked it in there, but I fucking

LOVE it out here! Right now. I might have let a few years get away from me, but it's okay. I believe everything happens as it should. Besides, my idea needed some time to bake and I needed some time to learn how to trust myself and follow the path life is already carving for me. A few of my favorite customers, who work at a bank, have always told me to see them if I need a loan in the future. And I've been saving money ever since I started working at The Cup, so everything is already working out as planned. Mmmmmm. Can you smell the Seabiscuits?

Well... *(awkwardly pausing for a moment)* Today is Sunday. It's just about 5 p.m. I have only a few moments left of my final mission at The Cup. The day I dreamed of is finally here, but it doesn't feel anything like I thought it would. Honestly, it doesn't really feel like... anything. I mean it's not like I'm going to leave here in tears, but I'm not going to backflip out of here, either. Instead, I think I'll dance out of here because that's what I love to do. So, for one last time as a Cosmos Coffee Cup captain, I want to tell all of you to have a nice voyage. It's only just begun. Mission Complete.

(Stars are projected all over the stage as Ronnie exits, dancing off. The screen changes to display a spiral galaxy. Blackout. End of play.)

About the Author

Aaron Pitre is a performer, playwright, and poet from Seattle, Washington. His path in the performing arts began when he taught himself to moonwalk in his grandmother's dining room. Pitre is a graduate of Suffolk University and the author of the poetry collection *Bleed*.

www.aaronpitre.com

About the Play

Inside the Cup was first performed at a juice bar in Hartford, CT in 2012, and published in 2014. This second edition has been updated to incorporate gender-neutral characters and language.